THE
SANTA CLAUS
BOOK

by Aurelius Battaglia

Formerly Titled The Reindeer Book

Golden Press · New York
Western Publishing Company, Inc., Racine, Wisconsin

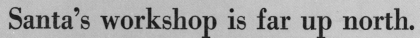

Santa's workshop is far up north.

Here is his house.

Santa is ready to start on his trip.

His sleigh is
packed with toys.

Here is one of Santa's reindeer.

Here is Santa starting off.

The owl and the bear

watch Santa go.

The bunny

and the raccoon
see him pass.

Here comes Santa,
high in the sky
with his eight reindeer.

The little town is covered with snow.

Santa has presents for everyone.

He puts them under the tree
and fills the stockings.

Everyone is dreaming
of a Merry Christmas!